That Nelson!
written by Tom Sullivan
illustrated by Anne Kennedy

Text copyright © 1995 by Tom Sullivan
Illustrations copyright © 1995 by Anne Kennedy
Designed by Russ Maselli

Published in 1995 by American Editions
150 East Wilson Bridge Road,
Suite 145, Columbus, Ohio, 43085 USA

American Editions is an imprint of American Education Publishing Co.

ISBN 1-56189-392-7
Printed in the United States of America

# THAT NELSON!

**TOM SULLIVAN**
Illustrated by Anne Kennedy
American Editions · Columbus, Ohio

"That Nelson!"

That's what people said whenever Nelson was around. It wasn't that Nelson meant to get into trouble. It's just that he was so curious that sometimes he couldn't help himself.

Nelson didn't just dig a hole in the yard. He kept digging to see how deep he could go.

Nelson didn't just smell the clothes that were hanging on the line. He had to taste them too.

Nelson didn't just feel the leg of a table. He had to see if his teeth could bite through the wood.

And then there were the cushions on the chairs. He had to find out what was inside them. That Nelson!

Of course, all ordinary dogs get into trouble now and then. But Nelson wasn't an ordinary dog. Nelson was supposed to be a special dog, a dog that would help blind people to be independent. If Nelson could just learn to put his curiosity to good use, he could become a guide dog someday. But it wouldn't be easy.

The place where Nelson got into the most trouble was the kitchen. On his first Thanksgiving, he spent all day smelling the turkey cooking. Every time he came in from the yard to visit the family he lived with, the smell made him drool. He knew that he wasn't supposed to eat anything from the kitchen counter, but when his family went away, Nelson just had to get close to that wonderful odor. He was so curious about where that odor was coming from that he began to shake all over.

And then it happened.

A little bit of the turkey gravy dripped right onto his nose! Now he just couldn't control his curiosity. He had a little taste of turkey. Then he had another. He ate and ate and ate. He ate until he was so full he waddled when he walked.

When his family came home, he was so full he couldn't even run to greet them. He had a terrible stomachache. But the stomachache wasn't as bad as what happened next.

"Bad dog! Bad dog, Nelson!" the father yelled.

"What are we going to do with you, Nelson?" said the mother.

"You've got to try harder, Nelson," said the little girl. "If you don't learn to control your curiosity, you're never going to get to go to the school for guide dogs."

Now Nelson felt so bad that he had an ache in his heart too. He felt so bad that he ached all over. He hadn't meant to eat the turkey. He just couldn't help it. He understood he had to do better. He wanted to please his family. He just didn't know how to do it.

Over the next few months, things began to change for Nelson. Instead of staying in the yard when the family went out, Nelson went with them in the car. He went on errands with the mother. He went to the office with the father. And he even went to school with the little girl.

Everywhere they went, he wore a jacket around his body. Whatever it was, it must have been special because people said things like, "Hey, look! Guide dog in training. Isn't that great?"

Nelson loved it. Now he could be curious all the time because there was so much to see.

11

But then one morning, the family drove him to a place where there were lots of other dogs. Nelson noticed that everyone in the family was crying. The little girl was crying the hardest of all. "I love you, Nelson," she said. "Be good to your new master."

"We're glad we could help you through your puppy time, Nelson," the father said. "You were a great 4-H project."

"Now you have to grow up and try to become a special dog for your new master," the mother said, sniffling. "You'll be taking care of someone now. You've grown up so much. Now you have to grow up even more."

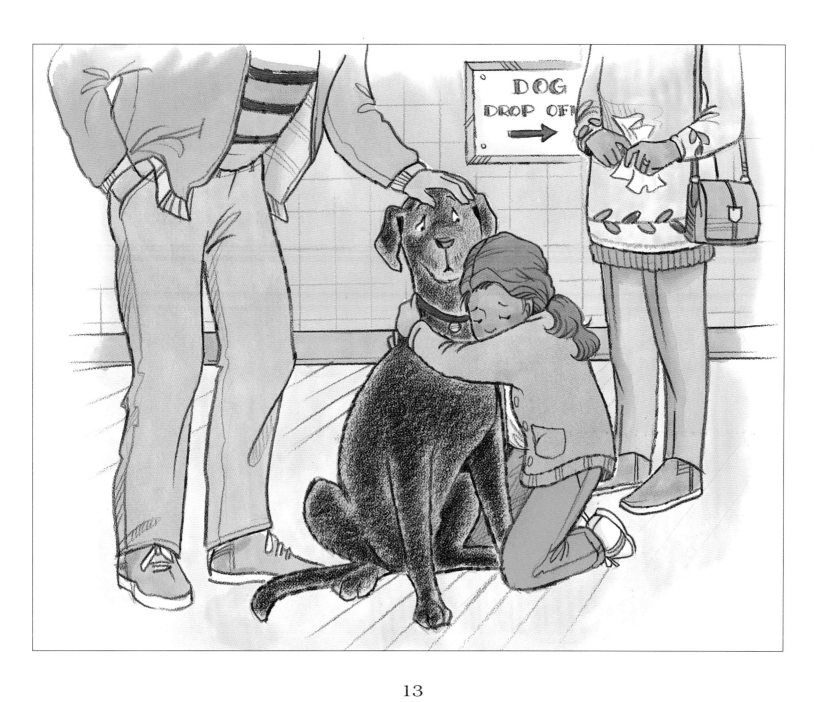

None of this made any sense to Nelson. All he knew was that he had been happy living with his family, even if he did get in trouble once in a while.

Now he was put in a place called a "kennel" with many other dogs. He liked dogs, but he liked people better. The first night in the kennel, Nelson couldn't sleep. He cried all night. Why had his family left him in this horrible place? Had he gotten into so much trouble that they didn't want him anymore?

The next morning a man came to the kennel gate and called his name. Nelson was curious. The man's voice sounded so warm. When he patted Nelson, his hands seemed to say, "You're a good dog and I'm very happy to meet you."

The man told Nelson that he was his trainer. He told Nelson that they were going to do some very important work. But first, he said, Nelson had to learn obedience.

Nelson had heard that word before from the family. It meant that he had to do what people told him to do. Being obedient wasn't much fun, especially for a curious dog like Nelson.

But Trainer's voice was so kind that Nelson decided to try. Every day after a big breakfast, Trainer would take him to a place he called "park." This is where all the dogs had to learn to go to the bathroom with their leashes on. Nelson was curious about why he had to do this, but he tried to do it anyway.

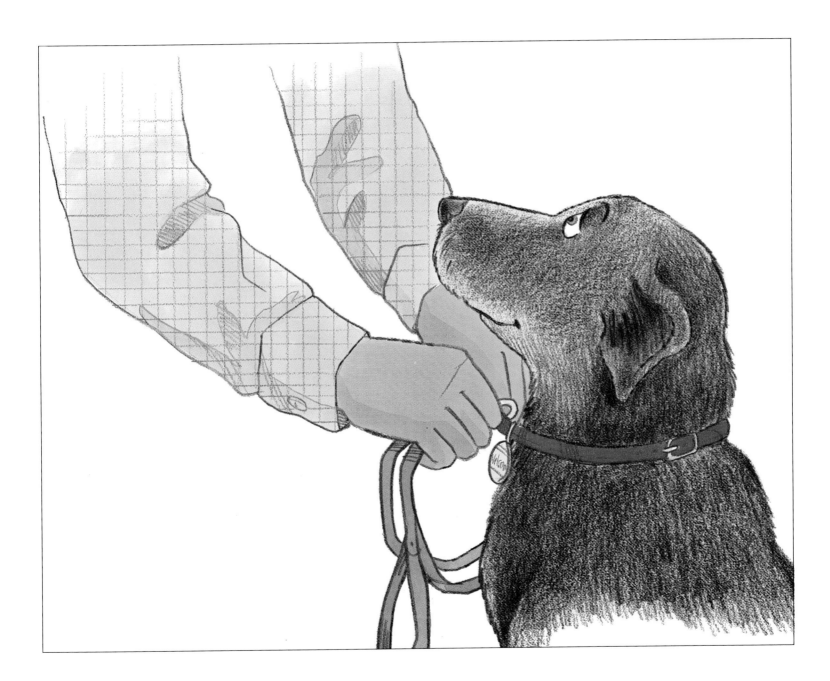

Then they would walk and walk and walk. Trainer kept saying things like, "Heel, Nelson." Nelson figured out what those words meant. They meant that he was supposed to walk right at Trainer's left side, never ahead of him and never behind him.

Trainer also told Nelson to sit and stay every time they came to the crossing of a street. Sometimes they would go into restaurants and Trainer would have food. Nelson could smell it. He was curious about what the food was. He was so curious that sometimes he just had to try it. That made Trainer angry.

"No, Nelson! " Trainer would say sharply. Nelson would feel that aching feeling in his heart again. That ache told him that he would have to try harder.

After a while, Trainer put this strange-looking new thing on Nelson's body. It had a strap that ran around his stomach and attached with buckles. A long handle ran down his back.

Trainer called this a "harness." He would pick up the handle of the harness and hold it in his hand and say, "Forward." But this time he didn't want Nelson just to walk next to him; he wanted Nelson to pull forward and lead. Nelson was curious again. Why was Trainer doing this? But Trainer kept encouraging him, saying things like, "Good boy! That's a good boy! Go ahead, Nelson, forward!"

Nelson liked this idea. He liked deciding where they went. But Trainer wouldn't let him go just anywhere. He commanded Nelson to go to certain places. He would say, "Find the door, Nelson," as they were walking down the street, and Nelson would have to go to the door of the next building that he saw.

He would say, "Find the elevator, Nelson," and Nelson would have to go inside one of those little boxes that goes up in the air. That scared him, especially when it was made out of glass and Nelson could see how high up he was.

He would say, "Find the chair, Nelson," and praise him every time he found an empty chair for Trainer to sit in.

The toughest one was when Trainer would say, "Nelson, find the curb." Then Nelson would have to place his feet right on the edge of the sidewalk where Trainer was going to cross the street. If he forgot to do this, Trainer would correct him. And Nelson learned never to go forward into the street when there was traffic. If cars were coming, Nelson learned to wait until it was safe.

Nelson was still curious, but now he was learning to control his curiosity. Controlling his curiosity meant that he was learning to use all of his senses to do the things Trainer asked him to do.

Nelson still got into trouble sometimes, but it didn't happen very often anymore. And he felt that aching feeling in his heart less and less.

Soon, the work he did with Trainer was fun. Soon, the work was more like a game.

One day when Trainer came to get Nelson, there was another man with him. The man was holding onto Trainer's arm and seemed very nervous.

"This is Tom," Trainer said to Nelson. "He's going to be your master."

*My master?* Nelson thought. *I don't want anyone else. I like Trainer!*

This man, this Tom, did not understand how to play the game Trainer called "work" at all. Why was he tripping on things? Why did he always bang into stuff? And why did he blame Nelson every time he hurt himself?

Nelson felt that ache again. He just didn't understand.

The man was very kind to Nelson, but Nelson still wasn't sure that he liked him. At night, Nelson didn't have to stay in the kennel anymore. He slept in a room next to Tom's bed in the special school where Tom was staying. Sometimes Tom let Nelson sleep on the bed. Nelson still wanted to be with Trainer, but it felt good to snuggle up to Tom. It almost made the ache disappear. Every day when all three of them worked together, Trainer kept saying, "Remember, Nelson, Tom's eyes don't work and you have to be his eyes. Pretty soon you two will be out in the world by yourselves and I won't be there. Tom is going to need all of your help."

Nelson didn't understand what Trainer was saying. He did begin to understand that every time he kept Tom from getting hurt or found just the place that Tom wanted to go, Tom was happy and gave him a lot of love. Though he still loved Trainer, after a while Nelson decided that maybe having Tom as a master might be okay after all.

One morning, Trainer came to get Tom and Nelson. Trainer told them that today was the day for their big adventure. Nelson was curious. He wondered what this adventure was all about.

He soon learned that he was to take Tom into the city to do all kinds of exciting tasks. First they went on the subway, an underground train. That scared Nelson because it made so much noise, but he took care of Tom anyway. They rode in taxi cabs from place to place. Nelson led Tom into hotels with lots of people and elevators. They even walked down the busy streets of the city where traffic whizzed all around them. It was a lot different from the small town where they had trained, but Nelson used all of his senses and did everything right – finding the buildings, stopping at curbs, remembering to be careful on steps, and finding chairs.

Everything Nelson did was perfect! Nelson understood that Tom was proud of him and that made Nelson so proud he felt he would burst. And Nelson could sense something else about Tom. He could feel that Tom loved him. And what was even more wonderful, was that Nelson knew that he loved Tom. The ache was gone. And for Nelson, it would never come back.

At the end of the day, Trainer said, "You did it! The whole day was perfect. Tomorrow, you graduate. Nelson, you will be leaving school. You'll be living with Tom now, helping him to have a new life—a life of freedom and independence."

Both Tom and Nelson felt wonderful, but they were tired, too. When he slept that night, Nelson slept a deep sleep knowing that he had done his best. He had finally learned to use his curiosity to do his job. He would be a guide dog after all.

The next morning, the family that Nelson had lived with came to the school to see him graduate. Nelson was so glad to see them! Everyone had brought him treats. There were dog biscuits from the little girl, special candies from the mother, and a juicy bone from the father. Nelson didn't take the treats, though. He didn't even drool, shake, or quake. He was doing his job.

Everyone told him how special he was. And, for the first time, Nelson understood why.

Now when people say, "That Nelson! He's so curious!" the feeling in the words has changed. They don't say "That Nelson!" because he's in trouble. Nelson is still curious, but now he's a special guide dog, sharing his life with his blind master.